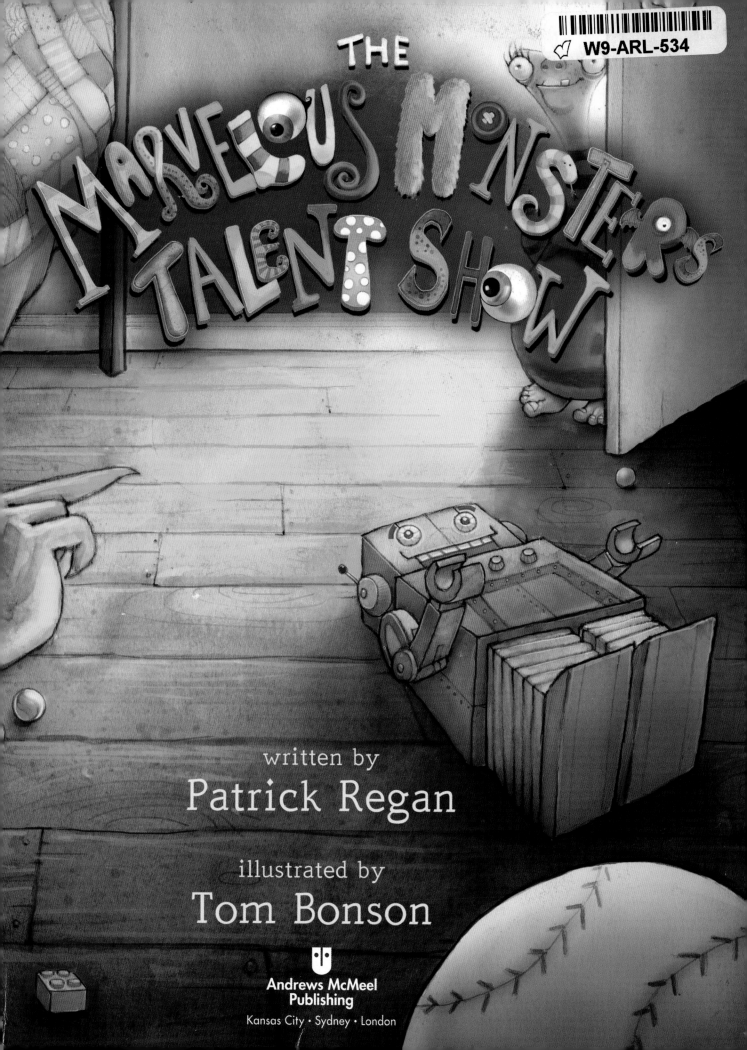

THE MARVELOUS MONSTERS' TALENT SHOW

written by

Patrick Regan

illustrated by

Tom Bonson

Andrews McMeel
Publishing

Kansas City · Sydney · London

Ladies and gentlemen, mutants and ghouls . . .
Welcome to tonight's performance of
The Marvelous Monsters Talent Show!

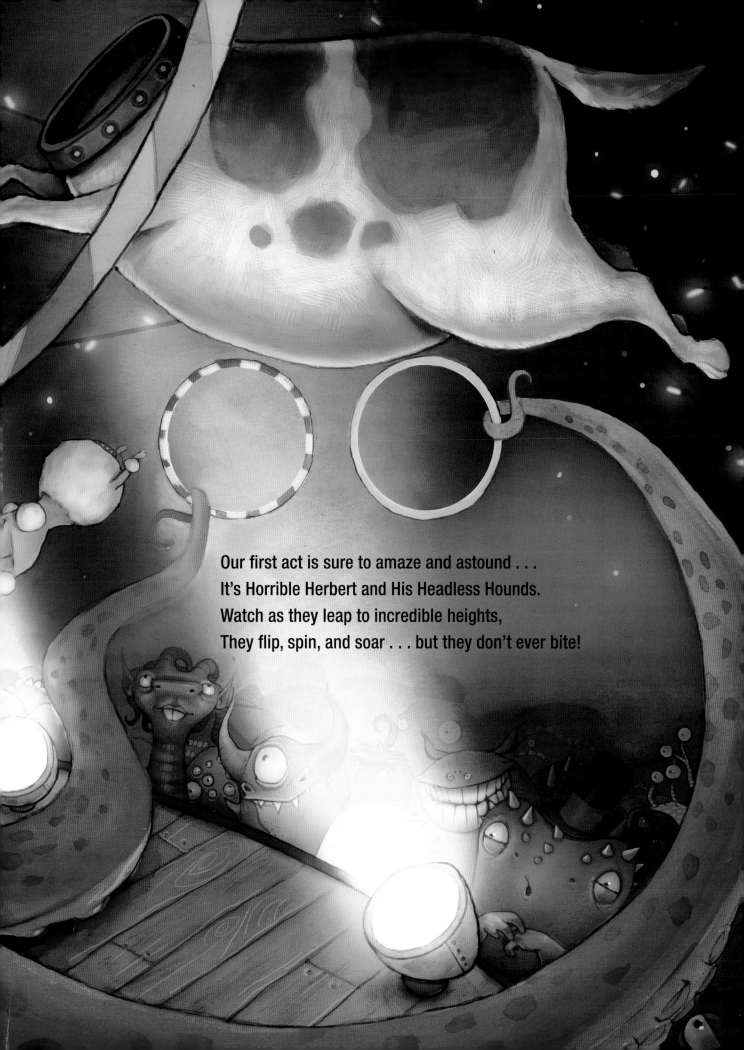

Our first act is sure to amaze and astound . . .
It's Horrible Herbert and His Headless Hounds.
Watch as they leap to incredible heights,
They flip, spin, and soar . . . but they don't ever bite!

Our next big act is REALLY huge!

Minnie the Muncher eats it all—
Fire! Swords! Bowling balls!
In France, she devoured the Eiffel Tower.
How's that for super swallowing power?

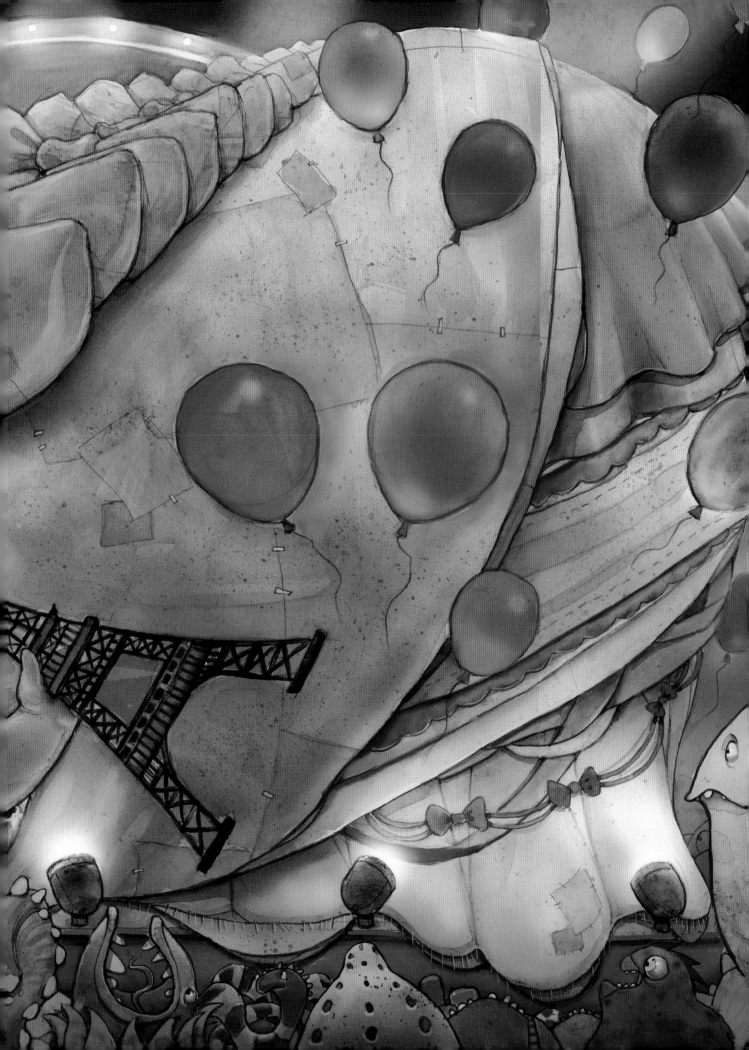

High above our stage, it's Cy and Wink.
They're terribly talented, don't you think?
On one wheel they wobble across the high-wire.
If I said this looked easy, would I be a liar?

Now kids, if you've ever tried to juggle,
You know that it can be kind of a struggle.
But Ollie the Ogre's such a pro,
He never misses a catch or throw.
Five balls in the air—such skill, such grace . . .
When he's done, he'll pop two back into his face.

Friends, the pool down below is just six inches deep,
But that fool on the platform is ready to leap.
He'll be down here with us in just two seconds flat.
Let's just hope he goes SPLASH, and doesn't go SPLAT!

And now for something truly wild . . .
It's See-Through Sal, the Invisible Child.
Performing his most incredible trick . . .
He's skipping rope on a pogo stick.
While bouncing and skipping, he's pouring hot tea!
Now isn't that a sight to not see?

Folks, here's an act you must hear AND see . . .
It's monster three-part harmony.
One head sings high, another sings low,
And the third doesn't quite know where to go.
By the time this talented trio is done,
You'll know three voices are better than one.

If you liked that last act, you're in for a treat.
It's Señor Snap and his fast-tapping feet.
With breathtaking speed he keeps seven feet tappy.
How about a big hand for this talented chappy?

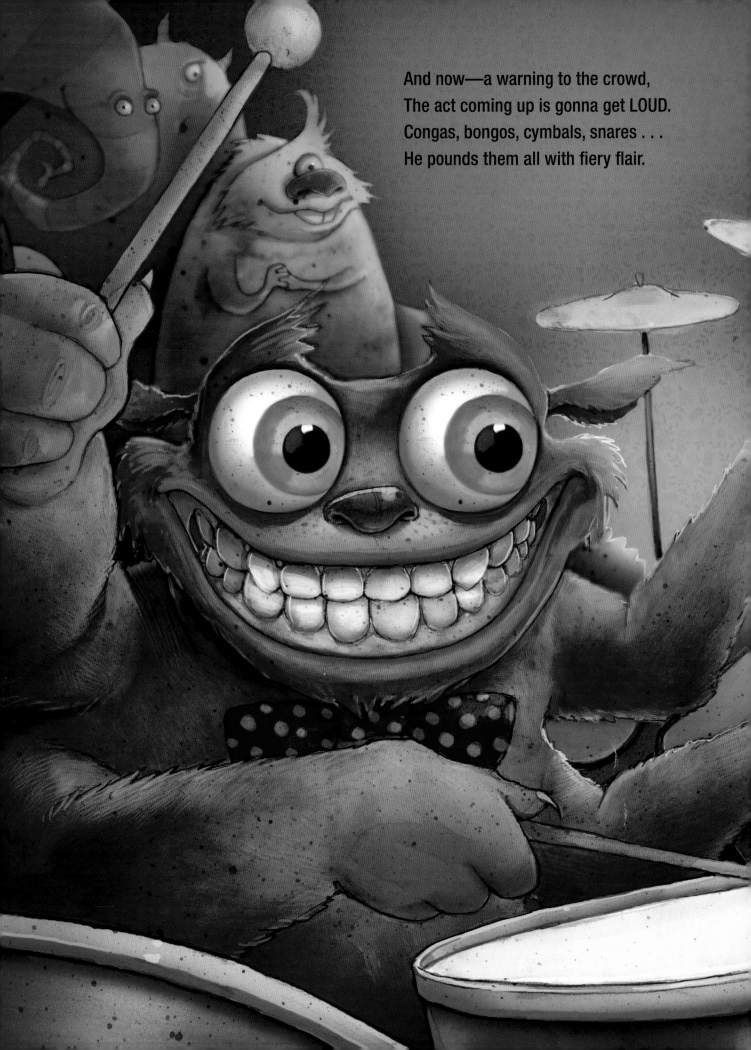

And now—a warning to the crowd,
The act coming up is gonna get LOUD.
Congas, bongos, cymbals, snares . . .
He pounds them all with fiery flair.

Wow! Now, that cat sure can play!
You don't see his kind every . . .

HEY!
Excuse me, guys—I should have knocked . . .
But this is a school night, and it's 8 o'clock.
That means quiet time upstairs.
You don't want Mom finding you in here.